Items should be returned on or before the last date shown below. Items not already requested by other borrowers may be renewed in person, in writing or by telephone. To renew, please quote the number on the barcode label. To renew online a PIN is required. This can be requested at your local library.
Renew online @ **www.dublincitypubliclibraries.ie**
Fines charged for overdue items will include postage incurred in recovery. Damage to or loss of items will be charged to the borrower.

Leabharlanna Poiblí Chathair Bhaile Átha Cliath
Dublin City Public Libraries

Comhairle Cathrach
Bhaile Átha Cliath
Dublin City Council

Brainse Mheal Ráthluirc
Charleville Mall Branch
Tel. 8749619

Date Due	Date Due	Date Due

50 Below Zero

Story by Robert Munsch
Art by Michael Martchenko

annick press
toronto • new york • vancouver

Thirty-fifth printing, July 2012

Annick Press Ltd.

We acknowledge the support of the Canada Council for the Arts,
the Ontario Arts Council, and the Government of Canada through
the Canada Book Fund (CBF) for our publishing activities.

 ONTARIO ARTS COUNCIL
CONSEIL DES ARTS DE L'ONTARIO

Cataloging in Publication Data

Munsch, Robert N., 1945–
  50 below zero

(Munsch for kids)
ISBN 0-920236-86-3 (bound).—ISBN 0-920236-91-X (pbk.)

I. Martchenko, Michael. II. Title. III. Series:
Munsch, Robert N., 1945–   Munsch for kids.

PS8576.U58F53 1986   jC813'.54   C84-098485-5
PZ7.M86Fi 1986

Distributed in Canada by:
Firefly Books Ltd.
66 Leek Crescent
Richmond Hill, ON
L4B 1H1

Published in the U.S.A. by Annick Press (U.S.) Ltd.
Distributed in the U.S.A. by:
Firefly Books (U.S.) Inc.
P.O. Box 1338
Ellicott Station
Buffalo, NY 14205

Printed and bound in China.

visit us at: **www.annickpress.com**
visit Robert Munsch at: **www.robertmunsch.com**

To Jason, Watson Lake
and Tyya, Whitehorse, Yukon Territory

In the middle of the night, Jason was asleep: zzzzz—zzzzz—zzzzz—zzzzz—zzzzz.

He woke up! He heard a sound. He said, "What's that? What's that? What's that!"

Jason opened the door to the kitchen ...

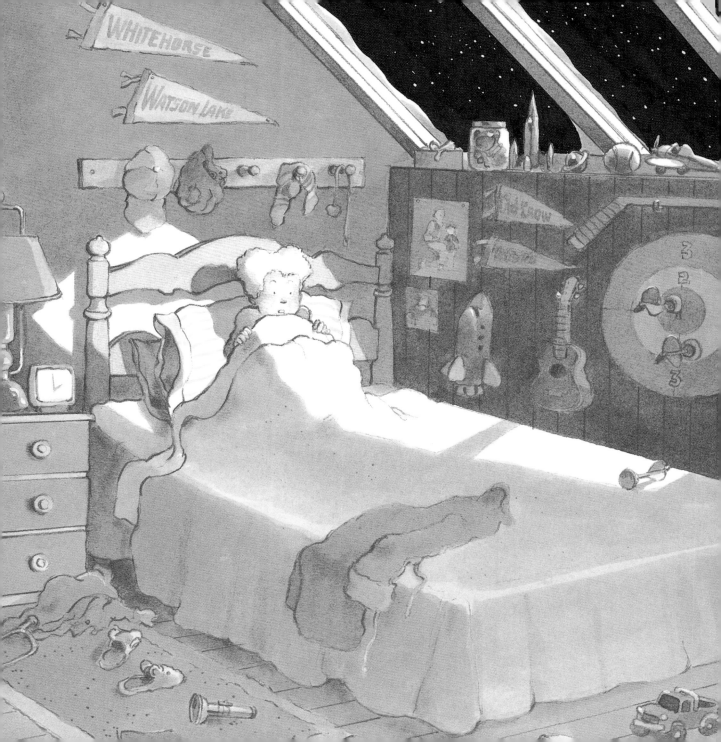

and there was his father, who walked in his sleep. He was sleeping on top of the refrigerator.

Jason yelled, "PAPA, WAKE UP!" His father jumped up, ran around the kitchen three times, and went back to bed.

Jason said, "This house is going crraaazy!" And he went back to bed.

Jason went to sleep: zzzzz—zzzzz—zzzzz—zzzzz—zzzzz.

He woke up! He heard a sound. He said, "What's that? What's that? What's that!"

He opened the door to the kitchen. No one was there.

He opened the door to the bathroom ...

and there was his father, sleeping in the bathtub.

Jason yelled, "PAPA, WAKE UP!" His father jumped up, ran around the bathroom three times, and went back to bed.

Jason said, "This house is going crraaazy!" But he was too tired to do anything about it, so he went back to bed.

Jason went to sleep: zzzzz—zzzzz—zzzzz—zzzzz—zzzzz.

He woke up! He heard a sound. He said, "What's that? What's that? What's that!"

He opened the door to the kitchen. No one was there. He opened the door to the bathroom. No one was there. He opened the door to the garage ...

and there was his father, sleeping on top of the car.

Jason yelled, "PAPA, WAKE UP!" His father jumped up, ran around the car three times, and went back to bed.

Jason said, "This house is going crraaazy!" But he was too tired to do anything about it, so he went back to bed.

Jason went to sleep: zzzzz—zzzzz—zzzzz—zzzzz—zzzzz.

He woke up! He heard a sound. He said, "What's that? What's that? What's that!"

He opened the door to the kitchen. No one was there. He opened the door to the bath-room. No one was there. He opened the door to the garage. No one was there. He opened the door to the living room. No one was there.

But the front door was open, and his father's footprints went out into the snow— and it was 50 below zero that night.

"Yikes," said Jason, "my father is outside in just his pajamas. He will freeze like an ice cube."

So Jason put on three warm snowsuits, three warm parkas, six warm mittens, six warm socks, and one pair of very warm boot sort of things called mukluks. Then he went out the front door and followed his father's footprints.

Jason walked and walked and walked and walked. Finally he found his father. His father was leaning against a tree.

Jason yelled, "PAPA, WAKE UP!"

His father did not move.

Jason yelled in the loudest possible voice, **"PAPA, WAKE UP!"**

His father still did not move.

Jason tried to pick up his father, but he was too heavy.

Jason ran home and got his sled. He pushed his father onto the sled and pulled him home. When they got to the back porch, Jason grabbed his father's big toe and pulled him up the stairs: *bump, bump, bump, bump.*

He pulled him across the kitchen floor: *scritch, scritch, scritch, scritch.* Then Jason put his father in the tub and turned on the warm water.

                                        glug.

                                 glug,

                           glug,

                      glug,

                glug,

The tub filled up: glug,

Jason's father jumped up and ran around the bathroom three times and went back to bed.

Jason said, "This house is going crazy. I am going to do something." So he got a long rope and tied one end to his father's bed and one end to his father's big toe.

Jason went to sleep: zzzzz—zzzzz—zzzzz—zzzzz—zzzzz.

He woke up! He heard a sound. He said, "What's that? What's that? What's that!"

He opened the kitchen door ...

and there was his father, stuck in the middle of the floor.

"Good," said Jason, "that is the end of the sleepwalking. Now I can get to sleep."

In the middle of the night, Jason's mother was asleep: zzzzz—zzzzz—zzzzz—zzzzz—zzzzz.

She woke up! She heard a sound. She said, "What's that? What's that? What's that!"

She opened the door to the kitchen and ...

Other books in the Munsch for Kids series:

Many Munsch titles are available in French and/or Spanish. Please contact your favorite supplier.